A Book

of Stories

For Children and Others

To Liam
Enjoy the stories!

Aaron A. Lehman

AARON A. LEHMAN

ISBN: 1482005018
ISBN-13: 9781482005011

The names of some characters have been changed to protect the identity of the person involved in the story. Other characters are entirely fictitious and any resemblance to the names of actual people is coincidental.

Acknowledgements

Dianne Tchir- Editor

Winifred Lehman- Proof reading

Illustrated by- Nicole Linfoot and Lori Snider

Richard Krikun- Bander in Charge at Lesser Slave Lake Bird Observatory

Nicole Linfoot- Assisant Bander at Lesser Slave Lake Bird Observatory

Table of Contents

Chapter 1
Tornado

"Tornado!" thirteen year old Sharon yelled to her younger brother Tim. Red headed Sharon was in charge of the home place, while Father and Mother went to the Simpson farm.

"Run to the machine shed!" her voice trailed off into the rushing wind.

Tim, Kal the farm dog, and Kandis the cat raced to the machine shed with its stone walls and weathered door. As they struggled to get to the security of the old building, the wind howled fiercely about their heads, and pushed against their bodies.

"Hurry, help me with this door," Sharon called. Her voice quivered with fear. "If we can get this door closed and bolted down we should be safe."

"Help me!" Sharon screamed to Tim. One last heave-ho and the door slid into place with the bolt secured. What a relief to be sheltered from the constant pushing of the wind. With the bolt in place, they could feel the security of the machine shed. Its massive walls were made of huge stones, taken from nearby fields over one hundred years ago. Cemented into place, they withstood the many seasonal storms of the past, and provided shelter now, even in the face of a tornado. The heavy beams overhead were fashioned from tall maple trees, cleared to make room for fields of corn and hay.

"Tim, look through this crack, up past the maple tree. I think that funnel shaped cloud must be a tornado. It's coming this way!" They could hear a low roar in the distance, like a huge freight train and yes, it seemed to be getting closer.

Sharon told Tim some of Father's stories about tornadoes that sometimes swept across the northern Indiana farmland. With everyone safe, her voice seemed less frantic. Having never seen a tornado before, Sharon felt she missed out on one of the most spectacular weather wonders.

"Did Grandpa build this shed?" Tim asked.

"Father says our great, great, grandfather built it."

Tim wanted to hear more about his great, great grandfather, but as the roar got louder and louder, Sharon sensed something missing.

"Where is Missy?"

"I don't know. I saw her this morning," Tim recalled.

Missy was the pregnant cat that wandered into their farm yard, and decided to stay. They all fell in love with the attractive cat, showing all the signs of a mother to be.

"Poor Missy," Sharon cried. "What if she had her babies and they are all outside in the tornado?"

"Can I go look for her?" Tim asked Sharon.

"No, we can't leave here until the storm is past."

Sharon looked through a crack, between two of the big stones, to see if there was any sign of the old, rust bucket of a truck that her parents took to the Simpson farm to check on some cattle. Sharon hated that truck! She hoped father would trade it off before she was old enough to drive. How embarrassing it would be to drive into town with the back fender flopping back and forth. She did hope it would keep Mother and Father safe during the storm. Kandis and Kal snuggled up to the children and they all waited as the roaring pounded their ears.

"Poor Missy," Sharon sniffled.

Screech! Crash! Bang! They tried to cover their heads as dust and dirt fell all around them.

"We must have lost the roof," muffled Sharon.

Dust was flying everywhere making it hard to see and breathe. As they dusted off their hair and clothes, Sharon and Tim began to cough. Eventually, the dust settled and the roaring noise faded into the distance.

Kal started barking at the door and then they all heard it. It was the rust bucket truck coming up the driveway with the fender flopping. What a pleasant sound.

"They're safe!"

"I want to look for Missy," Tim said.

Sharon strained to pull open the big door, and everyone went charging out to meet Father and Mother. They were fine, and sitting between them was Missy and her family of eight kittens.

"Missy! You fooled us," Sharon called.

"Now I don't have to look for you," Tim told Missy.

"Kal and Kandis will have lots of friends," Sharon noted.

Kal gave a bit of a bark.

Everyone was happy that they had survived the tornado.

"Thanks, Sharon, for taking care of the place," Father praised.

The tornado passed just east of the farm buildings and left a big path of twisted trees and fence posts. The only other damage they could see was a strip of roofing missing from the machine shed and the top of the windmill that was lying in the hay field. The machine shed was a safe place from the storm.

"Hop in," Father said. "We have to check on the Andersons. It looks like they may have been hit."

On the way, Mother told them how she found Missy and her family in a bale of hay on the back of the truck. As she unloaded hay at the Simpson place, Missy emerged with her whole family. Mother put them inside the truck to protect them from the wind.

What a storm! They were all safe.

"Now I'll be able to tell my own story about seeing a tornado," Sharon said, as she snuggled Missy and the new kittens.

Chapter 2
Puppy! Puppy!

Puppy bounced from one snow bank to another on this cold, blustery winter day. He ran up to a tall stately gentleman in a long black coat, wearing a black beret. He followed. He whined. He ran beside. He whined. He ran ahead. He whined.

"Stop following me!" the stately gentleman said. "Go home!"

Puppy continued on up the street bouncing from one snow bank to another. The wind was getting colder and stronger. He ran up to a short, stocky gentleman with a toque. He followed. He whined. He ran beside. He whined. He ran ahead. He whined.

"Stop following me!" the gentleman in the toque said. "Get lost!"

Puppy continued on up the street. He ran from one bush to another, smelling each one as he went. The wind was very cold and snow began to fall. He ran up to a lady with a cane, bent low in pain. He followed. He whined. He ran beside. He whined. He ran ahead. He whined.

"Stop following me!" the lady with a cane said. "Go away!"

Puppy continued on up the street. The wind was blowing snow into big drifts. He ran on the sidewalk. He ran on the road. A car had to turn quickly to miss him. He smelled food and followed his nose. He ran up to a group of teenagers. He followed. He whined. He ran beside. He whined. He ran ahead. He whined. He jumped to bite a sandwich. He missed.

"Get out of here!" the teenagers yelled.

He whined.

Puppy continued up the street. Snow swirled around his shivering body. He heard someone singing softly. He ran up to a young girl. She stopped singing. He followed. He whined. He ran beside. He whined. He ran ahead. He whined. He stopped in front of the young girl. She reached out to pet him.

"You must be cold," she said.
He shivered.
"You must be hungry."
He licked her hand.
"I'll take you home."
He jumped up and licked her face.
Leaping and bouncing, they ran for home.
"It's nice and warm in here."

He whined.

"Here, have a warm drink."

He gulped with gusto then licked her hand.

"I'll call this number on your tag."

Sometime later he heard footsteps at the door.

"Puppy! Puppy!" a little boy shouted.

He leaped into the air and smothered the boy with kisses. Kisses for everyone.

"Thank you! Thank you! You found my puppy!"

Chapter 3
Sammy's Snow Slider

"Sammy! Gordie!" Danny called. "Bring your sliders to the hill. The snow is great!"

Fresh snow covered the local toboggan hill.

"Let's try out our new sliders," Gordie said to Sammy.

Everyone had received new sliders for Christmas except Sammy.

"I don't have a slider," Sammy said in his high pitched voice. "You go ahead. I have to take this loaf of bread to Grandma."

"I never get to do any fun things," he mumbled as he headed away from the hill.

Pulling the hoody over his head and ears, he started thinking.

Grandma is sick and Mother works hard to help out. We can't afford things like sliders.

He smiled when he remembered how his sister Nellie laughed when she saw a teddy bear peeking out of her Christmas stocking.

I loved finding the beanie baby puppy in my stocking.

"I hate snow!" Sammy yelled as he kicked a big cardboard box lying in the alley.

"AARRGH!" he screamed as he gave it another kick and headed down the path to Grandma's house.

"Why so sad?" Grandma asked as she opened the door and took the bread. "Come on in Samuel and have a slice of toast with some of my strawberry jam."

Sammy loved Grandma's homemade jam, but he wanted a slider.

"I can't go sliding on the hill because I don't have a slider."

"So that's the problem."

"Gordie and Danny got new sliders for Christmas."

"This is a good day for sliding," Grandma agreed.

Jasper, Grandma's kitten was playing in a shoe box. Grandma gave the box a shove toward Sammy.

"There, see if you can cheer up Sammy while I make some toast."

Sammy loved kittens and Jasper was fun to play with.

"Hiya!" Sammy said as he gave Jasper a hard push.

Jasper went sliding along the floor and then flew out of the box as it tipped on its side.

"Here's your toast," Grandma said, handing toast loaded with jam to Sammy.

"There! Take that!" Sammy said as he gave Jasper another hard shove across the floor.

Sammy finished his slice of toast and watched
Jasper slide the shoe box around on the floor. He
was still a bit sad, but it was fun playing with
Jasper and Grandma.

"Box! Box!" Sammy squeaked. "I know how to
get a slider, Grandma. I can use a box!"

"That's a great idea, Sammy. We used boxes
for sleds when I was a girl."

"How did you do that?"

"We opened a cardboard box so we could sit on
it and hung onto the flaps. We could even steer it
by pulling left or right on the front flaps."

"I've got to go, Grandma."

"Why so soon?" Grandma wondered.

"Thanks for the toast and jam."

Sammy ran all the way back to the box in the alley. It was just the right size. He kicked and pulled it open, spreading out the flaps. Grabbing his homemade slider, he ran as fast as he could to the toboggan hill.

"Sammy!" Gordie called. "Why are you carrying that old piece of cardboard?"

"It's my slider," Sammy called back.

Everyone started making fun of Sammy and his cardboard as he pulled it to the top of the hill. When it came his turn, he grabbed the flaps of the flattened box and launched himself off the hill.

"Yiee!" Sammy screamed as he zigzagged, spun round and round and finally tipped into a snow bank at the bottom of the hill. What a ride! What fun! He had gone farther and had a wilder ride than any of the others on their new sliders.

It wasn't long before Gordie and Danny asked if they could try the cardboard slider. As the boys took turns with the cardboard, Sammy had a chance to try out their new sliders. It was fun, but everyone liked the cardboard slider best.

"Grandma, you're the greatest!" Sammy shouted as he launched himself off the hill one more time.

Chapter 4
Swords, Shields, and Race Cars

"Brent! Lizzy! Come Play!" David called.

Brent, David's younger brother and Lizzy his little sister, came running to the play area near the kitchen.

"Can we cut this cereal box?" David asked, as his mother prepared lunch.

"Sure, but be careful."

Brent and Lizzy were quiet for a change.

These are nice boxes. I'll make a sword from this one and we can play Roman soldiers, but Lizzy has the scissors.

"Lizzy! Bring the scissors here and we'll make something."

"No!"

"Brent! Take the scissors away from Lizzy. She'll cut herself."

"Waaaaa!"

Good she's crying.

"Mommy! Brent and Lizzy are fighting over the scissors," David shouted.

"How did you get those scissors? You can't have them, you're too little," Mother scolded as she came from the kitchen.

"Waaaaa!"

Good. Mommy put the scissors on the counter. I can reach them.

These scissors are really sharp. It's easy cutting the cereal box. I'll cut a long thin section and then tape on a cross piece to make a handle, but Brent has the tape.

"Brent, I need the tape," David demanded.

"No!"

"Lizzy, can you get the tape from Brent?"

"No! It's my tape," Brent yelled.

"Waaaaa!" screamed Lizzy as Brent shoved and tripped her.

"Mommy! Brent and Lizzy are fighting over the tape," screeched David.

Why are you two always fighting?" Mother asked with a sigh. "Give me the tape."

Good, David thought. *She put it on the counter.*

"Look Brent, this is my sword. Swoosh! Swoosh!" David yelled as he swung his sword through the air.

"Look Lizzy! Swoosh!"

"Waaaaa!" cried Lizzy when the sword hit her on the head.

Now I need a shield. I'll be a soldier. The front and back can come from another box. Arm straps. I'll cut them, thought David.

"Brent, will you hold this so I can tape it?"

"Okay. Will you help me make one?"

"Sure, then we can fight?"

"Look! Swoosh! Swoosh!" *I love the sound it makes as it swings through the air.*

Clunk.

"Waaaaa!" Lizzy's head seemed to be the target.

"Brent, I'll help you. Trace this with the pencil and then cut it out."

"This will be a big one," Brent said proudly.

"That's a good sword Brent. Now make a shield like this."

"Do you want one too Lizzy?" David asked.

"Here, I'll help you," he offered.

"Bring the tape Lizzy. This one is for you."

"Wow! We can have a big fight now," David exclaimed.

I'm going to make another sword. Maybe a helmet, thought David.

"Mommy will you hold this while I tape my helmet?" asked David.

"Sure," Mother said. "That is a great idea."

"Look Mommy, this is just like a Roman soldier. Swoosh! Swoosh!"

"Hey Brent!"

Smack! Smack! David's sword hit Brent on the head.

"Come on Brent, sword fight."

"Lizzy! Hit Brent!"

Swoosh! Swoosh! Smack! Brent's sword hit David on the head.

"Ow! Mommy, Brent hit me. I'm going to get you!"

Smack! Smack! The boys exchanged blows.

"Ooow!" David took another hit to the head.

It's a good thing I have my helmet on.

"Watch out Lizzy. Brent is going to hit you."

"Mommy, did real soldiers ever get hurt?" David asked.

"Yes they did."

"Ow!" David howled. "That hurt! Mommy! Lizzy poked me in the eye!"

Smack! "Take that." David said as he hit Lizzy on the head.

"Waaaaa!

I don't care if Lizzy cries and I'll trip Brent anytime I want. He's pretty tough though. I don't really want to hurt Lizzy, but she is such a pest pulling on my shield. Brent is a good shot! He can hit hard with his sword and it is bigger than mine.

"Brent! No more hitting! Let's put wheels on our swords. We can pretend they are race cars," suggested David, after taking another blow to the head.

"Lizzy, I'll race your car," David said. "Mommy, how fast can race cars go? Mine is going a thousand miles an hour!"

"Mine goes a million miles an hour," Brent countered.

"No, Brent, a car can't go a million miles an hour!"

"Let's colour our cars. Lizzy, go get the crayons. I get first pick. My car is going to be red."

"No, Brent, you can't have a red one. Mine is red."

"Mommy, tell Brent he can't have a red car because I said it first."

"Who would like to hear a story?" Mother asked.

"Me!" the children called at the same time.

"David," Mother said when the children were all seated around her, "I'm glad you changed your swords into cars. This story is about a young man named John, who was always telling others what to do and thought everyone should do what he wanted them to do. One day a man refused to be bullied by John and challenged him to a duel with swords."

"What happened," David asked.

"Well David, sometimes we need to think about how others feel and what they want to do. Think about that the next time you play with Brent and Lizzy," Mother suggested.

"Who wants to hear the story?"

"Me, Me, Me!"

Chapter 5

The Sugar Shanty

As I jumped from one dry spot to another on my way to the dilapidated sugar shanty, the cold, brisk wind forced me to bend forward, and grab my tattered, smelly barn cap. The sugar shanty was perched on a low rolling hill, overlooking a vast and winding river valley below.

"Don't get stuck in the mud," Mother called from the back door of the old two storey farm house.

"I'm a little man now, remember?"

I turned seven on my last birthday, and that makes me a man. I even go to school now. This will be my first time staying with Father as he works all night boiling sap in the sugar shanty.

The shanty was made of old weathered black and gray timbers from years of facing the blistering hot summer sun, and the brutal beating of northern New York thunderstorms. During many long, cold winters, these gnarly old boards splintered along their knotty edges by frigid sub-zero temperatures.

Creak…screech, the big sliding door on rollers at the west side of the sugar shanty opened. Part of the door was missing: sharp splinters stuck out where it had broken off. Inside the wood shed were piles of wood stacked in rows.

I remember the excitement, pushing the second wooden door on leather hinges open and billows of wet steamy fog blasting me in the face. Large hot pans of the evaporator rumbled furiously, as the sweet light maple sap boiled to make clear, brown, maple syrup.

"Hurry," Father called, as he tended the boiling sap with a big spoon that had a flat metal scoop and a long, splintered, wooden handle. "I'm going to need lots of help tonight." He wore thick heavy gloves to protect his hands from the splinters and the hot syrup.

I still feel the pain as a sharp sliver pierced the skin of my finger, and warm red blood oozed out.

The boiling sap frothed, bubbled, and gurgled as it flowed through the various troughs in the large metal boiling pan. On one side, sap dripped and trickled, thin and clear from the large, elevated, holding tank. Then it boiled and traveled across the pan to the other side where Father tested it. By now, most of the water changed to steam, producing the white fog that filled the shanty, and making it difficult to see.

"Come here," Father called. "I need your help to test this."

"How do I test it?"

"We use this big scoop and let the sap drip off the end. Here, put these gloves on, and you can try it."

"It doesn't drip," I said in a disappointed voice. "It just wants to stay stuck and slide along the scoop."

"That means the sap has turned to syrup," Father replied. "Open the spigot."

I pulled back on the hot, black, metal spigot attached to the side of the pan, and let the hot, brown, frothy syrup spill into a syruping off bucket, still sticky and gooey with dried crystals hanging on the edge.

"Okay, shut it off."

I pushed on the handle, and the flow of syrup slowed and stopped.

"Check the scoop. There is a bit left."

Father always liked to save a little syrup in the bottom of the scoop, and let it cool. It tasted so sweet as I sipped the warm, golden brown syrup and smelled the sweet, steam coming from the metal boiling pan. Sometimes, we made sugar on snow. Yum.

"Time to fire up." Father said. He walked to the front of the large, iron furnace. "Throw down some wood from the wood shed."

"Is that enough?" I called, after I pulled several heavy cut block logs from the wood shed.

"One more and that will be enough for now," called Father.

"Stand back," Father said as he used a long, black, metal poker to unhinge the heavy doors. The blast of hot air and bright light from the fire made me cover my face with my hands. Father grabbed long pieces of pine and maple from the wood pile and threw them onto the partially burned wood. The alternating red glow glistened with white ash and black cinders. With the crackling and roaring of the fire, I felt the intense heat and smelled the smoke as it burned my eyes and nose. After the new wood was piled inside, Father shut the doors with the poker, and the clang of the metal echoed throughout the shanty.

Wind started to rattle the loose metal sheeting on the sides of the shanty, and the tap, tap on the rusty metal roof told us a rain storm was coming.

"Grab this rope," Father instructed. "Pull hard!"

"I can't," I yelled. "It's caught on the pulley." The rope was hooked to a side door of the cupola on the roof. Father wanted to close it against the strong wind of the threatening spring storm.

"Okay, we'll pull together now." I pulled with all my might.

Finally the rope unhooked from the pulley, and the side door closed with a loud bang. It shook the shanty, but now I felt secure in the face of the storm.

"Get those eggs in the lunch bucket," Father instructed.

"How are we going to cook them?"

"Put them in the scoop and then roll them into the boiling sap."

Later, when the eggs had cooled, we cracked them open and had a warm, hardboiled egg with the sandwiches Mother sent along.

"This is the best sandwich I've ever had."

"Me too", Father agreed.

As the light of day faded into the gray and black of night, Father struck a match, lighting the old kerosene lantern with its long curved handle, and hung it on a rusty bent nail over the door. The wind caught a single flame flickering in its glass chimney and cast a long bouncing shadow across the steam laden shanty.

"Bed time," Father called. "You've had a big day."

I put some soft blankets on a bench near the stove, and the warmth of the fire; the crackling of the burning wood, and the rumbling of boiling sap sent me into a spring time, maple sugar dreamland in the sugar shanty.

"What a great day for a little man!"

Chapter 6

Chuckie the Woodchuck

Dive! Chuckie's brain screamed.

A four legged frenzied barking mass of a dog lunged toward Chuckie the woodchuck.

No time!

Back up and fight.

Woodchucks are known to be vicious fighters, slashing with their big teeth. Chuckie's instinct told him to fight.

Barking, snarling, slashing and then a sharp whistle.

That was close. I'm going home, Chuckie thought as the big dog ran to greet his owner. Chuckie retreated to his side of the fence.

I can't tell anyone about this because my parents warned me not to go across the fence into the neighbour's yard.

Home was a burrow along a fencerow with a hidden opening at each end. Chuckie, the youngest of ten woodchucks born to Mr. and Mrs. Woodchuck, always felt picked on.

"Chuckie," Mother would call. "Clean your room. Take out the garbage."

Green grass in a nearby park provided food for the big family. Mother and Father warned against going to the other side of the fence with big houses and a sign **BEWARE OF DOG.**

One day, while everybody was eating the park grass, Chuckie slipped away again to the other side of the fence.

This grass is so much fresher and crisper than on my side of the fence.

What's that?

A terrible noise came from a machine mowing the grass. Little people were bouncing up and down on a big blue blanket behind the big white house. They were laughing and screaming most of the time.

Pretty weird, but then, little people do a lot of weird things. Little woodchucks just eat.

Hide! Chuckie hid behind a rose bush as the lawn mower went by and then he headed for home.

I'm not scared. I know how to handle people and the dog from the big house.

That evening, Mother, Father and Uncle Bill told family tales of life on the other side of the fence. They issued a stern warning about going across the fence.

"I remember the hawk attack on Uncle Freddie Woodchuck," Father said. "He has never been seen since."

"Aunt Annie lost her foot in a gopher trap," Mother recalled.

"Did you hear that loud crack ringing through the fencerow just after sunset?" Father asked. "That was from a shotgun."

Uncle Bill told a sad tale about his Willie. "Willie had dug a burrow on the side of the fence toward the big white house. One evening, Willie came out of his burrow to eat grass in the yard. A man from the house was hiding in the fencerow with a shotgun. Willie was the last of the family to dig a hole on the house side of the fencerow."

All of the young woodchucks were shaking with fear, but not Chuckie.

I'm not afraid.

Chuckie recalled all of these stories as he peeked through to the other side of the fence, but over the next several days, Chuckie would sneak off and go farther and farther from the safety of the fencerow. One time, Chuckie spotted a different kind of grass.

This looks like the freshest and tastiest grass I have ever seen. I just have to try some.

Another fence. This fence has smaller holes than the one on the fencerow.

No problem. I'll just dig a hole under the fence.

Popping up through a hole on the inside of the fence, Chuckie couldn't believe what he saw.

Wow! What a place to eat! This is a real woodchuck cafeteria!

Chuckie started eating and ate until he was chuck full.

I can't wait to tell the others. Oops! Maybe I shouldn't tell anybody. I'd be in big trouble if Mother and Father found out where I've been. I'd better head for home.

Chuckie discovered that he had to dig his hole a bit bigger to fit through with his fat tummy.

At home in the nest, Chuckie went fast to sleep. No one seemed to notice that he had disappeared for a long time, or that he had a bigger tummy than usual.

One day, when Chuckie returned from the woodchuck cafeteria, Grandpa and Grandma were visiting. Grandpa had a limp because he was missing several toes on one foot.

"When I was a young woodchuck, I was captured by a person from the big white house and had to live in a small cage," he related. "I managed to escape, but my toes were bitten off by a big dog that chased me to the fencerow. I almost died," he exclaimed. "It's a miracle I'm alive today." All of the little woodchucks were shaking with fright, except Chuckie.

Ha. I know how to handle that dog.

On the next trip to the garden, Chuckie stayed longer than usual and ate an extra helping of special grass. While squeezing through his hole to start for home, the large, vicious, snarling, barking dog charged. Chuckie lost speed because of his fat tummy. He zigged and zagged trying to find a different path home.

"Help!"

No help.

I should fight him again, but now I'm too fat.

The dog grabbed him by the foot and bit off several toes. The pain seared through his body and blood spurted out of the wound. With a loud snarl the dog grabbed for his head, but Chuckie twisted loose by slashing with his teeth and hobbled into the bushes.

"Buster!" someone from the white house called. "Buster, you get over here! How did you get out of your fence?"

Chuckie licked his wounds, and hobbled along the fencerow.

Where am I? I've never been here before. It's getting dark.

I'm scared.

My foot hurts.

I'm lost!

Chuckie recalled Grandfather's story.

Maybe I'm not so smart.

What's that awful smell? I've never smelled anything like that before.

Choke! Choke! Gag! Gag!

I can't breathe.

His foot hurt, his tummy hurt.

Flames leapt into the air.

The fencerow's on fire and I can't find my family.

A flashing light from the flaming brush lit up the night sky, and a siren wailed in the distance. Flames leaped across the fencerow where Chukie was hiding, and he hobbled to a nearby ditch. As the scorching flames and searing heat passed overhead, he ducked into the water. After it passed, he popped his head into the air.

I'm alive. And I can breathe better!

Which way should I go?

"Chuckie!" Father called.

"Chuckie!" Mother called.

Chuckie heard the calls, and hobbled toward the sound.

"What happened to you?" Father asked.

"We looked everywhere for you and couldn't find you," Mother sobbed.

"Come on, we're headed to another fencerow. Our home is all burned out. We'll have to build a new home."

"What happened to your foot?" Mother wanted to know.

"I've got a long story to tell you later," Chuckie said as he hobbled along at the tail end of the Woodchuck family.

Chuckie decided that if he lived long enough to become a grandfather woodchuck, he would tell his grandchildren this story and would warn them to never go across a fencerow to the side with a big white house, where the grass was greener and seemed tastier.

Chapter 7
Billy the Bully

"Look out! Here comes Billy," Jim called.

"He failed last year." Lucy whispered. "I don't like him."

Our small town stretched the length of a long hill. I lived in an old two story farm house at the top of the hill, with my grade one to six school house at the bottom. Billy Schwarzenegger lived close to the cemetery on Second Street. Some days it took longer going to school than coming back home, especially if I didn't want to go to school. Sometimes it took longer coming home.

Billy's actions seemed to determine how I felt about school.

"He's sure older and bigger than everyone else in our class," Jim said.

"His father works at the factory, but the family is always poor," Betty informed us.

"Maybe it's because they have so many kids," Jim offered.

"Let's run," I said. "I don't want to get slapped."

"He always steals my hat," Betty said.

"He punches me in the stomach," Jim noted, as we all ran in different directions.

We never knew what to expect and we were petrified.

Since I was the scrawniest, weakest kid on the block, I usually got more punches than the rest. When I came home for lunch, I would often be crying or late.

Run! Hide in the cedar hedge.

He's gone. Safe to come out.

Late again.

My parents started to worry about me, and decided I should walk to school with my big sister when she went to work at the factory. This worked fine in the morning and noon, but it didn't work after school: I came home an hour before she got off work.

I hate going to school!

I hate the walk home worse.

Sometimes I would take a trail through our field behind the houses, but in the winter the snow was too deep. Even on Main Street, the ditches were filled with deep snow, and there was no escape. The fear of getting beat up by Billy was worse than the actual beatings and it upset my school work and my appetite.

I can't lose any more weight.

My parents always encouraged us to be non-violent, to love our enemies and do good to those who were bad to us. Well, I had done just about all the good I could to Billy.

I never bother him.

I just take his best shot and run home crying.

One day, my brother Jake, who was several years older than me, told me how he was also mistreated in school. His problem was a smaller boy who would jump on his back and kick him in the legs time after time, until his legs swelled up and became black and blue.

"Sometimes a bully needs to learn a lesson." he told me.

This should have made me feel better, but it didn't. Suddenly I realized, that if Billy was going to learn a lesson, I was going to have to teach him.

I'm scared! I can't do that! How can a scrawny kid like me handle a guy like Billy who is twice as big as me?

For several days I avoided Billy. I kept out of his way in the morning. I walked with my sister at noon, and waited around after school until Billy had gone home. Life was good. I could eat again.

Then, one day I miscalculated: I started for home, thinking Billy had already gone, but the teacher must have kept him after class and he was mad.

Oh no! I'm trapped!

I'm trapped between the big snow bank and the speeding trucks.

No place to hide!

Billy came charging up to me.

"There, take that," Billy sneered as he slapped me across the head making my hat fly into the snow bank.

"Ouch!" I cried as I doubled up in pain from a blow to my stomach.

But as his fist came toward my stomach the second time, I grabbed it and steered it to one side. As his big body came toward me, I lowered my bony little shoulder into his belly button and at just the right time I stood up.

"Woof!" Billy belched a groan.

To my amazement, big Billy went flying over my shoulder, feet flailing the air and crash landing in the snow bank, head first.

That was crazy! Now what is he going to do to me?

Before Billy could extract his head from the snow bank, my skinny little legs were running as fast as they could go. It was all up hill, but I think that was the fastest trip home I ever made.

Next morning, I was really scared.

"I don't feel good," I told my mother. "I think I should stay home today."

Just try it for the morning and see how it goes," she urged.

She had no idea what happened after school yesterday. I hadn't told anyone.

I tried every excuse I could think of to stay home, but Mother insisted I go to school.

At recess time my friends and I were building a snow fort and noticed Billy walking toward me.

Okay, I've had it now!

"You forgot your hat," Billy said as he dropped my hat at my feet.

No slap to the head!

No punch in the stomach!

Billy started helping build the snow fort and no one said a word.

"Wait up," Billy called as he came running up to me after school. "We can walk together."

Neither of us ever mentioned what happened the day before.

Billy actually became a very good friend of mine for the rest of the year and on occasion he would come to my house to play.

Chapter 8
Cops and Robbers

Bang! Bang!

"You're dead!" Ray yelled.

"No I'm not!" Rickie yelled back.

"I shot you!"

"No you didn't. See, I'm still walking around. You missed me."

"No I didn't. I shot you! Remember. I'm the cop and you're the robber. You're supposed to drop dead when I shoot you"

"I'm not a robber and I don't want to die!" Rickie said as the two boys walked toward each other.

"It's just a game," Ray reassured the younger Rickie.

"Why do I always have to be the one who gets killed?"

"Because you're the robber and I'm the cop."

"Well I don't want to be the bad guy anymore. I'm not a robber."

"It's just a game."

"I'm going home."

Ray and his younger brother Rickie often played cops and robbers around the small town neighbourhood, running to hide in the bushes or behind the big maple trees, pretending to shoot each other. When the games were played with cap guns early on a Saturday morning, all of the neighbours complained. Sometimes, when Rickie got tired of being the robber and didn't want to play anymore, Ray coaxed his younger neighbour Marty to play.

"Can I play hide and seek with Ray and Rickie?" Marty asked his Mother one Saturday morning. He was careful to specify that it was going to be hide and seek.

"Okay, but remember, no guns."

Marty's parents didn't think it was right for kids to run around pretending to kill each other, even if movie stars did it in the movies.

"I can play hide and seek," Marty called as he ran to meet the other boys.

"We're not playing that baby game," Ray announced. "We're playing cops and robbers. Rickie and I are the cops and you are the robber. And remember, when we shoot you, you have to fall down dead."

Marty knew he shouldn't play cops and robbers and he didn't want to be the bad guy who was going to get killed, but when Ray offered him one of his shiny cap guns, he just couldn't refuse.

"Okay," Marty said as everyone loaded up their cap guns with new rolls of caps, ready for action.

"We'll count to one hundred and then we'll come after you," Ray instructed.

Marty ran as fast as he could, and then found two overgrown bushes behind Mrs. Stamp's garage.

"Here we come," Ray shouted.

As the boys ran past his hiding place, Marty stayed quiet.

Wow! I'm safe, Marty figured. *I could have shot them, but I don't want to kill cops.*

Just then, Rickie caught a glimpse of Marty's shiny cap gun.

"He's over here!" Rickie called to Ray. "In the bushes."

Ray and Rickie ran toward the bushes with their guns drawn. Marty knew he was going to get shot and would be dead.

I don't want to die!

Marty didn't want to get shot, but he didn't want to kill anyone either.

In an instant, Marty jumped out of the bushes, grabbed his pistol by the barrel and let it fly through the air. The butt end of the gun caught Rickie right between the eyes.

Rickie screamed, and fell to the ground crying. Blood, mixed with tears from his eyes and snot from his nose, dripped from his head.

"Why did you do that?" Ray asked.

"I don't know," Marty said as he walked slowly to the scene of the disaster.

He started to cry and tears flooded his eyes. Caught up in the frenzy of the moment, and knowing he didn't want to die, he threw the gun.

Ray wiped Rickie's face, and they realized that the injury wasn't really all that serious. It was nothing more than a scratch and bruise he could have gotten when running through the bushes on a Saturday morning.

"I have to go home," Marty said. "Please don't tell my mother."

Relieved that Rickie wasn't seriously injured, Marty headed for home.

The boys never told their mothers what happened. However, the next Saturday, the boys played hide and seek. Killing cops or robbers wasn't such a good idea.

Chapter 9

Baseball at the Hay Lot

"Yay! School's out."

The clang of the hand held bronze bell chimed from the hallway as Mrs. Brewster waved it from side to side.

"See you tomorrow," Miss Moffatt called.

Bumping, jostling, poking, shoving, we made our way out the front doors of the four room school.

"Eddie!" I called to my friend who lived up the hill, close to our dairy farm located within the limits of our small town. "See you at the hay lot?"

Eddie waved back.

The hay lot joined Eddie's place with our farm, and the two of us spent many fun times there playing baseball.

Down the walkway I ran to the Main Street, glancing quickly both ways, and then hopping onto the sidewalk that led up the hill to our home. I was in a hurry to get to the hay lot, but I had some after school errands to run. Across the street, stood the tired looking general store with its big front porch, and heavy, double doors. There was no time to go in, and wish for a piece of candy from behind the cloudy glass counter.

Next to the store, a long building stretched out with its sloping metal roof, rusty looking siding and two separate doors. The side door opened to the post office. Inside, rows of mail boxes, and a window covered with bars, partially hid the Post Master. I could see Eddie, running up hill along the short cut.

I opened our mail box, and quickly pulled out the letters. I promised Mother I wouldn't lose anything this time.

I hope Eddie has some chores to do before he gets to play ball.

I still had to go to the hardware store to get some nails for Father. I opened the front door to the hardware store and went directly to the barrels containing different sized nails.

"What can I do for you, young man?" asked Mr. Hershey.

"My dad needs two pounds of eight penny nails. He'll pay later."

This is taking Mr. Hershey forever to fork out the nails.

Eddie will be home by now, and I'm still stuck in the hardware store.

I ran up the hill for home, and my body was invigorated as I breathed in the brisk fall air. The large Maple trees arching over the sidewalk, with their brilliant orange, red, and yellow colours, lifted my spirits. Reaching the top of the hill, I sprinted onto the level stretch, then up the driveway to the farmhouse with its sagging screen door, and sloughing white paint.

"Chore time," mother called. "Get your barn clothes on."

Oh no, I forgot about barn chores. Maybe Eddie will start playing ball with Larry, and then they won't let me play.

Running to the barn to greet my pet dog Brownie, a white mongrel with only one brown spot, gave me a welcomed break from the rigors of learning all day at school.

No time to waste on Brownie, I have to get to the hay lot.

"Throw down some hay for the cows," instructed my big brother.

Up the rickety ladder I climbed, into the gloomy cavernous hay loft. With a three tined pitch fork, I tossed hay over to the hay chute, and then dumped it down the hole to the hay manger below. I heeded the many vivid warnings about going too close to the hole. I didn't like the idea of having my brains splatter out on a manure covered concrete floor.

Through a crack in the side boards of the barn, I could see Eddie coming across the fence.

I'm going to be late, but I just have to jump onto the hay.

The excitement built as I climbed the inside of the barn from one beam to the next, and then shinnied across the middle beam suspended over the hay mow with its pile of hay many feet below. Cautiously I planted my feet on the beam, stretched my legs to stand up, and then launched myself into space. What a rush, free falling, and then bouncing into the soft hay with stems of hay, dust, and hay seeds enveloping my body as it sunk out of sight.

Out of the barn I raced, and yanked open the woodshed door. Grabbing the worn off, misshapen baseball, the scarred wooden baseball bat, and my flimsy, left handed ball glove, I sprinted for the hay lot.

"Finally, made it," I gasped. "And I bat first."

"No, I bat first," Eddie disagreed.

There was always an argument as to who would bat first, since the first batter could stay batting for a long time, while the other one had to chase balls all over the hay field. With just two players, one was the pitcher, and the lone fielder, and the other was the batter, and had to chase the wild pitches.

"Catch," I said as I tossed the bat to Eddie. "Hands up. Top hand wins." From where Eddie caught the bat, we alternated hands until he had the last full hand on the top of the bat. This meant he was the first batter, and end of the argument.

Eddie was a good batter, and by the time I could run to the field to get the ball; chase him around the bases, he would make a home run. I wasn't having fun chasing balls. Eddie would place hit the balls to my left or right, then over my head. It took me a long time to find the ball in the tall grass.

Just hit a pop up, and I'll catch it for an out.

No pop ups. I couldn't get him out. He was having great fun.

One time, I chased him to the makeshift home plate and tagged him out.

"Yay, now it's my turn!" I shouted.

"I'm not out," Eddie scoffed. "You missed me."

"You're out," I yelled. "I got you first."

"No way," Eddie scowled.

"Okay," I pouted, as I grabbed my ball and bat, and headed for home.

"Okay," Eddie said. "You can bat."

Too late. I headed for home; my head boiling in anger. Eddie scooped up his ball glove, and climbed over the fence.

Later that night, I had trouble sleeping.

Why did I get so angry?

What if Eddie gets mad at me, and won't play ball with me anymore?

In the morning, breakfast went down very slowly, and the walk to school seemed longer than usual.

If Eddie won't be my friend anymore, I'll never have anyone to play ball with again.

Eddie ran ahead of me up the school walk, but he turned in time to see me wave.

Ring! Ring! The bell summoned all students to go to their classes.

I hate school.

I was the last one to go to class.

From across the hall, a door opened and Eddie stuck out his head.

"See you at the hay lot," he called.

"Okay. You can bat first."

School just looked a whole lot better.

Chapter 10
Bubbles

A flurry of activity erupted from the locker room of Rockport Junior High Swimming Pool. The noise was deafening, as Glen Bishop timidly worked his way to a locker at the far end of the room. Glen, a tall skinny boy, had pimples on much of his face, especially on his oversized Roman nose. Dark, medium length hair covered large protruding ears, but his toothpick arms and his long legs with bucket feet attracted attention like magnets, especially in swim trunks.

"Hey skinny Bishop!" Jed Engler yelled to get Glen's attention. "Hey guys! Look at Glen. A real swimming hunk for the girls."

The noisy room turned to boisterous laughter as Glen became the target of Jed's teasing. Actually Jed was the swimming hunk, and all the girls tried to sit close to him at lunch time.

I hate school and I hate swimming, Glen thought to himself.

He had to be here today because this was the day to jump off the deep end of the pool.

If I don't jump off the deep end of the pool, I will flunk swimming class and coach said there will be no exceptions. I'm never, ever going swimming again!

"Hey Bishop!" Jed taunted. "You know there are two kinds of swimmers: floaters and sinkers. You look like a sinker to me. Ha!"

When coach blew his whistle, signalling time to shower and to get to the pool, the taunting stopped. Amid more teasing in the shower, Glen tried not to think about what Jed had said, but he couldn't help it.

I'm not a sinker! I know how to float!

Glen lined up with the other boys at the side of the pool. Some were using the diving board, but not Glen. As coach blew his whistle, indicating time for the next boy to jump, Glen cringed. He watched in awe as Jed made a perfect dive from the diving board, expertly splitting the water with minimum splash and gracefully emerging from the centre of the pool.

"Go ahead," Glen said to the boy behind him.

Glancing in the direction of the coach, Glen noticed he wasn't even paying attention, just blowing his whistle and writing in his book. Occasionally he would look up when one of the swimmers did a belly flop, splashing water in a million directions. However big the splash, every swimmer came floating to the top and eventually climbed out of the pool, shaking water from his head and tipping it to drain water out of his ears.

I don't want to be the only sinker!

All too soon it was Glen's turn.

The whistle blew, and with a last gasp of air, Glen gently let the force of gravity pull his long body, feet first, into the water. The cold water swirled over his tense body, and tightly closed eyelids, then swished up his nose and gurgled into his ears. He started kicking his feet, getting his body to level off, but it wasn't happening. He forced his eye lids open, and the caustic chlorinated water stung his eyes and blurred his vision. It was then he realized the problem.

My cursed big feet are planted on the bottom of the pool, he screamed to himself. *Oh no! I'm a sinker!*

To his dismay, he was standing on the bottom of the pool looking up. When he tried to kick his feet, he simply started walking around through the water.

My lungs are bursting! If I exhale now, I'll never get to the surface in time to catch fresh air.

Even now a tiny stream of bubbles started leaking out of his mouth and he could see them rise to the surface.

Jed was right! Glen screamed in his brain. *I'm a sinker! I'm going to drown!*

With the thought of drowning came the overpowering urge to survive.

I don't want to die!

Get to the surface!

Push against the bottom with all of my strength.

Push!

Up! Up!

Splash. His head broke through the water barrier.

Get to the side!

Swim!

With arms swinging and legs flailing, Glen was getting nowhere.

Scream!

No time to scream!

With his head quickly disappearing beneath the swirling water, all he managed was one desperate gasp as gravity became stronger than his muscles and his body began to sink.

When he opened his eyes, he once again found himself standing on the bottom of the pool. His situation was getting desperate.

Did the coach notice?

Does anyone know that I sunk?

In another attempt, Glen bent his legs and pushed with all of his strength.

Push!

Splash!

Kick!

Level off!

Grab the side of the pool!

Again, gasping and splashing his arms and legs, he felt gravity pulling him down for the third time.

I'm a sinker, but I'm not going to drown!
Walk uphill along the bottom.
Get close to the edge.
Push off one more time!
Grab the edge and hang on!

As Glen burst through the surface with his arms and hands desperately searching for the edge of the pool, he felt another swimmer beside him.

"You're okay," Jed said with a clear steady voice. "Reach over here to the edge and grab on."

Jed noticed the petrified boy struggling for life. He helped Glen out of the pool and comforted the trembling, skinny framed boy, coughing up water, spitting and crying all at the same time.

"You'll be okay," Jed reassured. "Just breathe deeply and not too fast. Here put this towel around you and dry off. You look gross!"

"Thanks for the help," Glen said in a shaky voice. "I really thought I was going to die."

"You know," Jed said thoughtfully, "I had only heard of people who were sinkers, but now I've seen one for myself."

"I could use a hot shower," Glen admitted. "I'm glad I have dry clothes in the locker."

"You know what?" Glen said as the two boys headed to the locker room. "I'd jump into the deep end again, if I knew you were the life guard."

"Guess what? I'm going to pass swimming class!"

Chapter 11

Marooned on Dog Island

It was a hot afternoon in late August and the boys slipped away unnoticed for a last bike ride to the lake before school started. What a great way to spend a lazy summer afternoon.

"Yippee!" Donald shrieked, as he splashed into the clear, cold water. With white sand curling around his toes, he waded into the shimmering ripples. After the hot bike ride from town, Lesser Slave Lake, a beautiful Northern Alberta lake, felt extra refreshing today.

"Come on in!" he yelled to his younger brother Ricky. "Don't be a sissy. Bert will never find out."

Bert is Rick's father and they are both Caucasian; Bert is also Donald's step father, since Bert married Donald's mother Mary, a Métis, making a family of mixed Aboriginal ancestry.

"Come on Ricky, climb on my shoulders and I'll throw you in." Donald, a dark haired thirteen year old, was much bigger and stronger than his blond ten year old step brother. Time after time, they threw each other into the rolling waves of the waist high water. Ricky struggled to lift Donald on his slender frame, and quickly became exhausted.

"You're such a weakling," Donald chided. "Come on, head for the beach."

Pulling themselves up out of the water, the boys sprawled out on the warm sand. It felt good to soak in the caressing rays of the warm summer sun.

"Snack time," Donald called.

"Great!" Ricky responded. "I'm starving."

"You look it! Ha!"

"Look!" Donald shouted, pointing along the beach. "What's that floating?"

The boys strained to see a dark green blob floating toward them.

"A canoe!" Donald recognized it first, but both boys were surprised to see an empty canoe drifting slowly by. "Let's grab it and go for a ride!" he yelled as he splashed with his big feet, in an effort to capture the run-away canoe.

"Bummer! No paddles. Come on in. Don't be chicken," Donald teased. "We don't need paddles. We can just use our hands to move around."

"That won't work," Ricky complained.

"Okay, here is a big stick we can use."

"Father wouldn't like it," Ricky said. "We shouldn't be stealing a canoe and besides, we don't have any life jackets. Father doesn't even know we're here," Ricky whined.

"Father! Father! That's all I hear," Donald taunted. Bert is your father, but he's not mine and I don't have to listen to him! I never liked him much anyway and he's not going to run my life!"

"I know he likes you," Ricky offered. "You should give him a chance."

"Why should I?" Donald snarled. "Come on get in, or are you going to be Father's baby again?"

"Okay," Ricky replied timidly, "but don't go too far from shore."

"How did Dog Island get its name?" Ricky asked from the bow of the canoe, pointing to the small, somewhat rounded island a few kilometres from Devonshire beach.

Donald always had answers for Ricky's questions, even if he had to make them up.

As the boys floated leisurely along the beach in the pirated canoe, Donald started his answer.

"Well, I heard the Elders talking about that one time. In the olden days, the trappers and the police used dog teams for transportation in the winter. During the summer, the dogs were kept on the island so they couldn't run away. That's how it got its name."

Because Slave Lake is one hundred kilometres long, fifteen kilometres wide and only fifteen metres deep, weather conditions can change quickly, producing white capped waves in a matter of minutes. The boys were relaxing in the canoe, and failed to notice the tell-tale signs of a major storm brewing in the east. Thunder heads billowed high above the scraggly Jack Pine trees on the sand dunes, and a strong wind blew the canoe away from shore.

"Paddle!" Donald screamed. "Paddle! The stick won't reach bottom and we're over our heads."

The boys leaned over the side of the canoe and splashed with both hands, but they were still drifting away. With the strong wind, the waves became higher, and the innocent ride in a stolen canoe was becoming a nightmare: a roller coaster ride on the white capped waves on an angry lake.

"We shouldn't have come," Ricky whimpered above the splashing and thumping of water on the battered canoe.

"Oh shut up!" Donald yelled back. "Keep paddling!"

Ricky was nearing exhaustion and Donald would soon give up as well. They could no longer hang onto the gyrating canoe: bucking like a bronco at a rodeo, the canoe was now completely out of control.

Clouds darkened the sky. A pall of gloom hung over the lake as darkness engulfed the boys. The raging water tossed them into the air, and they bounced hard on the gunnels along the side of the canoe.

"Hang on!" Donald yelled to Ricky. Ricky's panicked eyes were bulging from their sockets.

Ricky was losing his grip on the canoe. Just then, with a crashing blow, a huge wave swept over the boys hurling them into the churning water.

"Grab the canoe!" Donald yelled between fits of sputtering water and gasping for air. He kicked his powerful legs and swam toward the escaping canoe.

"Ricky!" Donald yelled. "Where are you?"
I can't find Ricky!

Panic crept into his chest as he thought about losing Ricky.

I can't lose him!

He loved his brother, even though he was Bert's baby. And Bert?

Bert is a good father and I usually start the arguments. Should have listened to Ricky. I'll change my attitude. I don't want to die! I don't want Ricky to die, either!

Donald suddenly realized how much he loved his family.

"Ricky!" Donald yelled once again, into the darkness.

No reply above the pounding of the waves.

Desperately searching for his brother, Donald finally grasped the edge and pulled himself toward the overturned canoe.

As his legs kicked under the canoe, they struck a body.

Grab for the body! his brain screamed. *Ricky is drowning! I can't hang on!*

Just as both boys were being sucked to their death, in the cold, swirling, frothing water, Donald kicked against a rock.

"Bottom!" he shouted, as he made a last desperate lunge for Ricky.

"I touched bottom! Hang on!"

Slowly, Donald bounced his way along the rocks, dragging Ricky and the canoe toward shore, fighting the wind and the waves in the black of night.

"Cough! Cough! Choke! Choke!"

Both boys were coughing and spewing water.

That's a good sign. Ricky's still alive!

"Swim Ricky! Swim!" Donald yelled through the gurgles of water.

As the water became shallower, the boys were able to half walk, half crawl on the slippery rocks.

At last Donald pulled the swamped canoe up onto the rocks and both boys spit the last of the lake water out of their lungs.

"I think this must be Dog Island. Those lights in the distance are from Slave Lake. It's a good thing we hit the island or we would be drifting for another hundred kilometres."

"I'm scared." Ricky began to cry. "Are we going to have to stay here all night? What about the dogs?" Ricky sobbed.

"It's okay. We'll be safe," Donald reassured Ricky. "No one can look for us until daylight. Besides, there aren't any dogs on the island anymore." Donald tried to act calm, but he was scared too and then a shivering spasm attacked his body

"Come here Ricky. Help me get this canoe up to the trees."

Rain poured down as Donald and Ricky positioned the canoe up-side down under the dense, overhanging spruce branches. With no matches to build a fire, it would be a long, cold night.

No matches, but at least we're alive!

The moss under the thick branches was still dry. Donald piled some under the overturned canoe and the boys crawled in. In the pile of moss, the boys began to dry off. Snuggling close to one another, their body heat helped to keep them warm. Finally sleep calmed the scared, weary boys.

During the night, the storm passed, and daylight broke across the island.

"Wake up!" Donald called as he rolled past Ricky. "I hear a motorboat!"

Indeed, several motorboats were trolling back and forth across the lake.

"Over here!" the boys screamed, as they stood up flailing their arms.

They both charged down to the rocky shore, waving and screaming frantically!

"They spotted us!" shouted Donald, when the lead boat turned in their direction. As the boat came closer, the boys recognized Bert.

"Father!" Ricky yelled.

"Father!" Donald yelled.

Bert leaped from the boat, and splashed toward the boys. He gathered them both into his arms as only a loving, caring father would do.

And both boys hugged their father, as only rescued, loving sons would do, knowing they would have a lot explaining to do.

Chapter 12
Trainload of Trouble

"See you in class," Drew called to his best friend Roy.

"I want to beat the train," Roy yelled back, as he jumped on his bicycle and headed for school.

Drew ate the last bite of his lunchtime sandwich, as he dashed out of the Boardwalk Restaurant, running to beat the train at the railroad crossing. His baseball cap was turned backwards over his long black hair, and his oversized tee shirt shouted **NO FEAR**. His baggy pants hung loose over his untied Reeboks. He spent too much time bragging to his friends about the new tricks he could do on the skate board half-pipe at Big Pipe Park. Everyone left for school without him.

I'm going to be late.

With long loping strides he headed for the crossing, but to his dismay a slow freight train blocked the crossing.

No problem, Drew told himself. *I'll have just enough time to take the shortcut across the railroad bridge and beat the fifth period bell.*

He didn't want to be late for class. That would mean a detention.

I have to be at Work Experience immediately after school and set up the new skateboard display at Sports First.

Drew had lots of ideas for his display at the sport shop, but they would have to wait.

"Help! Help!" someone yelled.

From a distance Drew recognized his friend Roy.

"Help me!" Roy screamed.

As he headed along the shortcut, Drew picked up speed. He could see Roy and his mangled bicycle caught in the rigging of a flatcar. Holding on for dear life, Roy screamed again. Raymond recognized the predicament of his friend.

Somehow, when Roy was attempting to cross the track, the rigging on the flatcar caught the front wheel of the bicycle. Now, he and his bicycle were being carried along with the train.

Drew didn't know how long Roy could hold on, but he knew he had to take action to save his friend from serious injury.

"Hang on!" Drew tried to yell above the noise of the train and the blowing whistle.

The train slowed down, going through town, and Drew knew what to do.

I'll gain momentum by running alongside, and then I'll grab onto the frame of the car in front of Roy. I can climb back to his car, and help him hold on. We can jump off at the school crossing.

Drew knew if he didn't do this perfectly, he could break his fingers, and be pulled under the screeching wheels of the train. With one final stride, and a kick of his powerful leg, he grabbed for a cross bar and swung onto the train.

"Help!" Roy screamed in pain.

"Hang on. I'm coming!"

Just then Drew realized how dangerous this was going to be. If Roy stayed where he was, he would smash head first into the fast approaching end of the railroad bridge and be killed instantly. Drew's **NO FEAR** tee shirt began to shake with fear as the adrenalin started to pump throughout his body. With steady feet, trained on the skateboard, he manoeuvred across the linkage between the two cars, first one foot then the other.

"Help!" Terror rang through Roy's voice.

Getting loose would mean rolling down the embankment to the river below, and that could end in death.

"Hold on!" Drew yelled as he lunged forward to grab Roy by the arm, and with his last bit of energy pulled him to safety. A split second later, the flatcar thundered across the bridge. The bicycle hit the end of the bridge, and bicycle projectiles went flying in all directions, some landing in the river.

The boys huddled on the flatcar, and Roy started to cry. They both realized how close they had come to death.

Drew's heart rate returned to normal, and then he heard the fifth period bell. He realized that he was going to be late for class. He also realized that the train was starting to speed up and head out of town. Before they knew it, the flat car passed the school crossing and they were headed for Smith. No one noticed the boys on the train.

"We have to jump!" Drew yelled above the screech of the train whistle.

"See those cattails up ahead? That should be a soft landing. On the count of three, jump as far as you can and roll."

Drew counted to three, and then delayed jumping himself, just to make sure Roy actually jumped. Both boys jumped as far as they could, and then rolled. There was a big splash with cattail fluff flying everywhere.

"We made it!" Drew laughed.

The boys checked each other out, and everything seemed to be in the right place.

"We're lucky to be alive. How did you get hooked up with the train?" Drew asked.

"I tried to beat the train, but couldn't. I tried to stop, but skidded into the flatcar and got hooked on the bar. Thanks for saving my butt."

"Puke!" Drew yelled. What is that terrible smell?" Then reality hit him. "This is an old sewage lagoon!" he yelled.

The boys were a sight to behold. They had sewage everywhere. Drew had sewage up his nose, in his ears, and he was soaked in it. His **NO FEAR** tee shirt was sagging from the weight of the sludge and cattails. His baggy pants were leaking water, and his baseball cap was floating next to a lily pad.

The boys looked at each other and burst out laughing. They were in big trouble, but they were alive. They would miss their afternoon classes and Drew would miss Work Experience at the sports shop. Worse yet, they would have to explain this mess to their parents.

"Come to my place," Drew offered. "We can spray off with the garden hose and then dry off in the back yard."

Drew was happy to be alive, and able to walk home, but what a stench. He would never forget this train load of trouble or this smell.

Chapter 13

Louis David Riel

Dream about what happened in
St. Boniface (Winnipeg, Canada) 1854

Louis! Louis! Father called.

Louis David was a ten year old, mop haired, brown eyed boy, and he didn't want to leave his secret hiding place. Hiding among the shimmering blades of grass along the bank of the Seine River, Louis hunkered down with his dog Raoul.

The Seine River flows through St. Boniface into the Red River, and is now a part of the city of

Winnipeg, Manitoba. The Hudson Bay Company named it and it was destined to become part of a new nation called Canada. Many people, including Louis Riel Senior, David's father, a devout French Catholic, did not want their Red River colony to be taken over by immigrants, who were primarily English and Protestant.

Louis! Father called again, his voice rising above the splashing sounds of a giant water wheel that powered a mill to grind grain into flour.

I'm not going, Louis said as he stroked Raoul's long, soft nose with saliva hanging from the one side of his mouth. The friendly dog blinked in agreement.

Louis Riel Senior married and moved to the Red River Settlement. As leader in the community, he helped Red River traders become free traders, and separate from the Hudson Bay and Northwest Companies. He was known as the 'Miller of the Seine', because he built and operated the flour mill for settlers in St. Boniface, a Métis outpost. The family history included a French fur trader, a Dene Aboriginal woman, and many relatives of mixed ancestry called 'Metisse' in French or Métis. Although Louis Senior was Métis, he helped all people of the Settlement including Aboriginal, French, Scots, and English. Most spoke French and followed the Catholic customs and religion.

Louis! Louis! Come here right now!

The eldest in a family of eleven children, Louis David was born in the Red River Settlement in 1844. He learned how to hunt and trap from his parents, and discovered the family history from the elders. Louis attended a school run by the Grey Nuns of the Roman Catholic Church, and, in spite of the negative comments about his Aboriginal ancestry, he excelled in his studies, impressing Bishop Tache. When Louis turned fourteen, he went to Montreal to study to enter the priesthood. All expenses were paid for by the Bishop. One time on a holiday, Louis traveled by Red River cart to visit his father, who was on a buffalo hunt in what is now Minnesota. This was the last time he saw his father alive. The early death of his father caused Louis much pain.

Louis! The surveyors are coming and we have to move this pile of grain! Father demanded.

I hate the surveyors, Louis snarled. Raoul's eyes drooped in a sympathetic pose.

The English surveyors were dividing the country into big square sections. The river-lot farms of the Red River Settlement, sectioned into long narrow strips, ensured that each farm had access to the river. The Riels and others were going to lose their land by the river under the new system. Louis and Raoul would no longer be able to come to this secret spot by the river.

Someday, I'm going to help my people get their land back, Louis told Raoul.

Come on, Father needs us. Raoul, you keep an eye on the surveyors, Louis commanded.

Just then a large beaver swam ashore. Boy and dog dropped down and lay perfectly still in the cool grass. The sleek animal shook his head and body, spraying water in all directions, and splashing Louis's face and Raoul's eyes. Soon the slimy beaver slithered over Louis' legs.

Reality 1885 Regina, Saskatchewan

"Aarrgh! Aarrgh!" Louis screamed as he awakened from his dream. "Get away from me! Let me out of here! I can't stand it anymore."

Now a grown man, he was lying on the cold prison floor of the Northwest Mounted Police near the present city of Regina, Saskatchewan. He realized the sound of the water wheel was rain splashing into his cold, wet cell. The beaver was actually a rat with slimy fur crawling over his legs.

Again Louis slipped into a dream.

Dream from events in 1860

Louis! Louis! Father called from somewhere in a herd of stampeding buffalo.

That's not possible, Louis thought in his dream. *Father is no longer living!*

Louis loved his father and followed his advice to get a good education, but after the death of his father, Louis quit preparing for the priesthood and began drifting from job to job in Canada and the US. After returning to Red River Settlement, Louis rallied the people against the Eastern Canadian government. He was instrumental in the creation of an army; the establishment of a provisional government, and in 1869 he took over Fort Garry, the Hudson Bay headquarters. Conflict between the two government forces resulted in Louis fleeing to the US, and being banished from Canadian Politics.

*Louis! F*ather called again amid the rumble of the buffalo herd.

Over here! Louis yelled.

In Dakota Territory, thousands of buffalo had been rounded up and Louis was riding his horse at break-neck speed through the stampeding herd. Louis lowered his gun and guided his horse beside a young animal. Its thundering hooves pounded the ground. A blazing blast from his gun caused the animal to fall beneath the surge of hooves. Later, Métis women came with large wooden carts and prepared the meat and hides for the settlement. Louis loved the excitement of the hunt, but most of all he loved the dried buffalo meat called pemmican.

Dream of events in 1875

Louis! Louis!

Is that you God?

In 1875, Louis had a vision that God had anointed him as 'prophet of the new world'. He now considered himself the voice for his Métis people, and chosen by God. His mental state became severe, and he was committed to a mental institution in Montreal. This stigma followed him to his death.

Louis! Louis! An angelic voice called from the Missouri River, Montana.

The angel turned out to be Marguerite Monte whom Louis married in 1881 and with whom he had two children. A third child was born, but died while Louis was in prison. In Montana, Louis enjoyed teaching at St Peter's Catholic mission. During this time, the Métis left the Settlement in Red River, and moved farther west to pursue the dream of a Métis country in, what is now, Saskatchewan.

Reality 1885

Rumble! Rumble! Screech! Screech!

"Aarrgh! Aarrgh!" Louis yelled with echoes bouncing off the prison's stark, gray walls.

"Let me out of here! I am not a traitor! I am a leader of my people, appointed by God!" Louis yelled over the noise of the Red River carts now gathering outside of the prison. The Métis people were coming to support their leader, Louis Riel.

Again Louis slipped into a dream.

Dream of events in1878

Rumble! Rumble! Screech! Screech!

Louis Riel! Louis Riel!

Once again my people are forced to move. Oxen are pulling the rumbling and screeching Red River carts northwest. How can my people survive the winter? They have no food and the buffalo are gone!

Dream of events in1884

Louis! Louis!

This time the call came from the Saskatchewan delegation in 1884. They convinced Louis to come back to Canada, organize the people, and present their grievances to the Canadian government. Several events, including armed conflict at Duck Lake and the final defeat at Batoche in 1885, led to Louis's arrest and charge of treason.

Reality 1885

Louis! Louis!

Louis heard the call coming from outside the prison walls. They were calling to let him know that they loved him and came to be with him in his final hour.

"I have failed my people!" Louis cried.

The rebellion against the Government failed. Many people died in battle, and he was blamed.

"I'm no traitor! I will die to help my people!"

The lawyers for Louis pleaded innocence by way of insanity, but Louis's final speech convinced the jury that he was mentally responsible for his actions. He was sentenced to death by hanging in Regina on November 16, 1885.

"Louis! Louis! You are our hero!" the Métis cried.

Louis dreamed of a day when he and all of his people would be honoured for their part in building the great country of Canada.

Sources used:

* A Biography of Louis Riel. University of Missouri-Kansas City
* Archives and Special Collections. University of Manitoba.

Chapter 14

Sir Ferdinand and the Fishy Tale

"Dive!" Sir Ferdinand shouted to all of the fish in Professor Popovich's thirty gallon fish tank, located at the front of the Science Lab. "Dive! It's the big eye of a land monster. Swim for your life. Hide in the ship wreck."

Just then there was a tremendous splash and a long appendage grabbed for Sir Ferdinand.

"A miss! Wow! That was close. Just brushed a bit of my tail," Sir Ferdinand said as he squished his bulgy goldfish body inside the old shipwreck, half sunken into the gravel on the bottom of the tank.

Professor Popovich had knighted Sir Ferdinand last year because he was the oldest fish in the tank, and had survived the misfortunes of the other fish. His nickname was Ferdie.

"Where is everybody?" Ferdie asked Sissy, a fragile nervous guppy, and the only other surviving fish in the tank.

"They all got caught by the land monster," Sissy said. "I think the monsters place bets on who can swallow us whole."

"I sure miss Pleco Plecostomus," Ferdie said plaintively. "He always cleaned up the tank. It sure is getting slimy around here without him."

"Psst! Hey Ferdie!" It was a land monster looking into the top of the tank with two big eyes piercing the depths. "It looks like Popovich is giving a tough lesson on refraction today," the land monster said. "Can you help us understand what he says?"

Sir Ferdinand often listened to Professor Popovich's complicated lectures and then interpreted them into language easily understood by the fish population. Apparently, some of the land monsters were listening in and taking advantage of his easy lessons.

"This sounds like a friendly land monster," he told Sissy, who was still shaking and shivering in a dark corner of the sunken ship.

"Don't go out! You'll be swallowed like the others," she warned.

Poking one bulging eyeball between the broken slats of the shipwreck, Ferdie timidly asked, "How can I help you?"

"From time to time I'll come by to sharpen my pencil. You give me your simple version of the lesson and I'll share it with my friends."

Before Sir Ferdinand had a chance to reply, Professor Popovich started sputtering something about homework. There was a rush of land monsters past the fish tank, but no splashes.

All was quiet and dark overnight, but Sissy and Ferdie were rudely awakened in the morning with bright lights and monster activity all around.

Screech! Scratch! Scratch! Professor started writing and drawing on the blackboard.

"Oh no!" Sir Ferdinand complained. "Here comes a cloud of chalk dust. We'll have to go white water rafting again."

"I hate it when that stuff gets into my gills," Sissy bubbled. "It takes me days to get clean."

"If I'm going to help the friendly monster, I'd better start listening," Ferdie figured. He could hear Professor talking about yesterday's lesson on linear magnification.

"$m=H_i/H_o=d_i/d_o$ and $P=1m/f$" Professor muttered as he scribbled equations on the blackboard and proceeded to stand directly in front of them. Sir Ferdinand could just see by peeking between a crusty old bucket and a pile of dusty books.

"If you have any questions, see me after school." It was Professor's usual offer to help, but no one wanted to stay after school. "Today we are going to learn about another phenomenon of light, called refraction. Blah! Blah! Blah!"

Sir Ferdinand peered through the side of the aquarium and could see many of the land monsters sitting at laboratory benches. Some were completely confused, some sleeping, some laughing, and others throwing paper airplanes toward the fish tank.

"Look out! A bomber!" Ferdie yelled to Sissy.

"Psst! Hey Ferdie! What's this junk about linear magnification?" It was the friendly land monster again.

"Well," Sir Ferdinand said, "if you look into a mirror, the size of your face in the mirror depends on how far your face is away from the mirror. The magnification of the image is proportional to the distance of the object from the mirror. The closer, the bigger, the farther away, the smaller."

"Wow! That's simple. Thanks Ferdie," he said as he disappeared toward the pencil sharpener.

More scratching came from the blackboard. Professor Popovich continued the lesson on light.

"Refraction is the bending of light that takes place at a boundary between two materials, having different indices of refraction. It is due to a change in the speed of light as it passes from one medium to another. The ratio of the sine of the angle of incidence to the sine of the angle of refraction is equal to the ratio of the velocity in the two media. Willebrord Snell is credited with the discovery that the sine's of the angles of incidence and refraction stand in constant ratio to each other. sinø i (incident)/ sinø r (refracted) = n We call this Snell's law. If light is traveling from a less refractive medium to a more refractive medium, (n2>n1) the refracted ray will be bent toward the normall."

"Snell's smells! Blah! Blah! Blah! Psst! Hey Ferdie! We're in big trouble. We'll have a quiz on this stuff tomorrow and we're lost. Sunk!"

"Well," said Ferdie, "think of it this way. If air and water had the same density, light would travel through both at the same speed. You could look at me and I would be exactly where you see me, since the angle of reflection and refraction would be the same. However, since water is denser than air, when you look at me in the water, I am not exactly where you see me. The angle of reflection and refraction are not the same. I'm actually lower in the water than I appear to you.

"Wow! That's amazing! You are the greatest Ferdie. Thanks a zillion!"

Ring! Ring! The class was over and the land monsters were zipping past the fish tank.

The Big Eye returns!

"Dive!" Sir Ferdinand yells.

Too late! Splash! A big appendage with five stumps plunged toward Ferdie. This time there was no escape. The five stumps clamped around his body and lifted him out of the water, into the land of the monsters.

Gasp for water! Work the gills! No good. Can't get oxygen from the air. I'm a goner.

Land monsters gathered around and one yelled, "swallow him!" Another called, "down the hatch!"

Sir Fedinand was thrust into a monstrous cavern with sharp white teeth all around. A big slimy tongue gave off a horrible stench. With a last ditch slap of his tail, Sir Ferdinand struggled for freedom.

Smack! The friendly land monster hit the bully monster on the back. As the bully coughed and gagged in revulsion, Ferdie flipped out of the smelly cavern and splashed into the fish tank.

Ferdie was almost gone, but soon revived when his gills made contact with the water.

"Dive!" Ferdie yelled to Sissy, but Sissy was already quivering in her hiding place in the darkness of the old ship wreck.

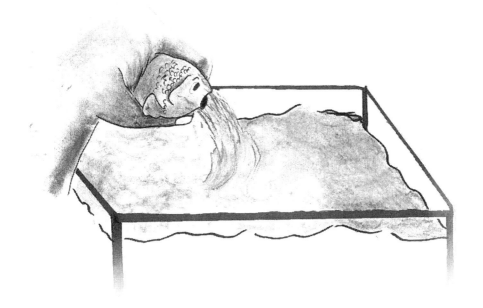

I should have never given my secret to the land monsters. Before, the big appendage would miss me because I was never swimming where the monster saw me. After the lesson on refraction,

he compensated for the bending of the light and was able to find me.

"Hey Ferdie!" the friendly monster called. "Are you Okay? I fixed that bully! He won't bother you again. Say, your ideas about refraction worked great. Next time I'll be more careful about sharing your lesson."

"Thanks," Sir Ferdinand said. "Maybe there won't be a next time."

He wasn't sure he wanted to do any more translations of Professor Popovich's lessons. It was too dangerous!

Chapter 15
Silo Boy

(For older readers)

As Tom climbed the last step to the top of the silo, pigeons fluttered into flight, soared over the farm yard and landed on the barn roof. The morning sun ushered in a sweltering day. Early this morning, Tom grabbed a stale bun from the pantry and headed for the barn. He threw some corn to the chickens, silage and hay to the cows and dumped the slop bucket into the pig trough. Soon after, he climbed the steel, half rusted ladder to the top of the silo.

Tom, a twelve year old orphan boy, often came to this perch high in the silo to be by himself and try to sort out his mixed up circumstances and the wild swings of his emotions. Under the soiled barn cap, his dark hair stuck out and the letters GLF (Grange League Federation) were printed on the cap brim. His brown eyes had a sunken, faraway look that comes with not knowing your real parents, and being circulated from one relative to another, or one foster home to the next. This one was going to be better. The old woman had promised she would take good care of him, since she could never have children of her own. It looked promising, even though the place was a bit run down and the food was skimpy at times. Joyce, as she called herself, was a bit plump, square jawed in the face with blue eyes, graying blond hair and a tender voice when talking to Tommy, as she called him. Things changed when the old man returned.

From his bed in the attached lean-to off the pantry, he often listened to the high pitched screams of the woman and the low pitched bellowing profanity of the man. He would cover his head to lessen the shrill screams.

Now looking through the broken, half window at the top of the silo, Tom viewed the farm yard;

scanning the barn roof with the pigeons, past the farm pond, to the broken down tool shed and then the weathered clapboard house with its well and storm cellar. A tall man, hunched over with torn coveralls pulled a bulging, over-sized garbage bag out of the cellar and dragged it towards the well. Viewing with a mixture of serenity and horror, Tom knew he was an innocent witness to something that caused his stomach to churn and would change his life forever, yet he couldn't be sure what it was.

I have to get out of here!

Tom slid part way down the rusty ladder, catching his hand on a metal sliver. Blood spurted out and dripped onto his shirt and pants, blending in with the patches of stain from cow manure and pig slop. A handful of silage at the bottom of the ladder helped soak up some of the blood and stop the bleeding.

Get to the hay loft. Now!

Tom climbed the old half broken, wooden ladder two rungs at a time, then crawled into the hay loft.

The pigeon nests.

The old man insisted that the only way to control the pigeon population was to smash the eggs. He also showed Tom how to wring the necks of the babies, if some had already hatched. Tom couldn't do that and had taken a few cuffs to the head for being such a useless sissy.

Could he do this to Joyce, or me?

Hugo prided himself in being a real man. His days in the mines made him tough and ready to deal with any situation. He had a face of steel, full of partly shaven whiskers and his slightly stooped posture hid his tall, well- muscled frame. His dark eyes could penetrate clean to the soul. He hated this wimp of a twelve year old who was always getting in his way. About all Tom ever heard from him was, "Do your chores or I'll wump you one."

"Boy! Where are you?" Hugo's voice rang out. His right overall strap swung from side to side as he walked into the barn. His cap covered his partly bald, graying scalp.

The loud, rough bellow echoed through the barn and scared the pigeons on the roof. They soared again around the farm yard and returned to the silo roof.

"Boy! Get out here and do your chores."

Tom started down the hay loft ladder to the dim lit cow barn stable below. The heat and humidity of the mid-summer day produced a river of sweat that poured down his face and soaked into the already blood stained shirt. Fumes from the manure filled gutter rose and blended with the stale odour coming from his sweaty body. The cows were now in the pasture, but the pig pen had not been cleaned in days and the chicken roost sported a hefty pile of droppings. Holding his breath, he turned to face the old man.

"Where were you?" the old man yelled.

"I-I-I w-w-was s-s-smashing the p-p-pigeon eggs l-l-like you showed me," Tom stuttered.

"What'd you seed this morning by the house?"

"I-I-I s-s-seed n-n-nuttin."

"Spit it out kid! What'd you heerd last night?"

"I-I-I h-h-heerd nuttin."

They both knew he was lying.

"One word from you and they'll be dredging the pond for you, you skinny bag of bones. Now get out of here and start cleaning the pig pen," he yelled as he cuffed the boy in the head, causing his hat to fly into the gutter.

Later, from the pig pen, Tom saw a newer model, red Lincoln pull into the driveway and a slender, middle aged lady, with high heels and a short dress walk toward the house. She knocked on the door and called for Joyce with a loud, but distinguished sounding voice. She went inside for a bit and then came out and looked around the yard.

"Joyce! Hugo!" she called.

Her blond hair swung to one side as she turned her head to look at the tool shed. Tom ducked low behind the big sow. Hugo was nowhere to be seen.

"Joyce! Hugo!" she called again and then got into the car and drove out of the driveway onto the gravel road, the windows closed tight keeping out the dust and the air conditioner on high providing relief from the heat.

A bulletin concerning Hugo's threat to kill Joyce appeared in the Sherriff's Office and when she missed a meeting with her sister, she was listed as a missing person. The sheriff decided to check it out.

As the Sheriff's car came into the yard, Tom could hear hammering coming from the tool shed. He threw some bedding into the pig pen and then went to the well for a drink. He worked the pump, but his suspicion prompted him to take a look down the well. What he saw churned his stomach like it was in a tornado. The contents spun round and round and then erupted, spewing puke in every direction. Her hair was floating over her face, yet a slight grimace peeked through the gray strands.

"Anybody home?" the Sheriff called out. "Hello!"

"What do you want?" Hugo snarled as he walked in from the tool shed. "Some people have to work, you know."

Tom pulled himself over to the big maple tree and leaned up against the trunk. His head was still spinning and his stomach churning, but he felt a bit better sitting in the shade.

"I'm glad you're working," the Sheriff drawled, the smile under his hat masking the intent for the meeting. "Somebody has to pay me to work on a hot day like this. My name's Chad. Someone called and said a woman from this place is missing. You know anything about her."

"Haven't seen her today," Hugo reported. "She's been pretty low lately. Maybe she ran off again. She does that every now and then."

"Hey kid," Chad yelled to Tom. "Have you seen the old woman lately?" Chad asked, the slight bulge over his belt signifying too many days behind a desk.

"No point in asking him," Hugo announced. "He's deaf and dumb."

Just then the lady in the air conditioned car pulled up and she and a friend with a camera walked toward the others.

"Have you found Joyce yet?" she asked.

"Not yet," Chad answered. "Hugo said she was a bit down lately and may have run off again."

"I'm her sister Eve, and she never runs off without letting me know where she is going. She must be around here somewhere."

Hugo's steel face and penetrating eyes glared at Tom and he knew enough to keep his mouth shut, but he walked to the well and pointed down.

Chad and Eve looked into the well and complete confusion ensued. Eve screaming. Chad trying to secure the site and Hugo trying to act sad and remorseful.

I'm outa here!

Tom slid behind the big maple and sprinted along the hedge leading to the pantry. He climbed through the window of the lean-to, pulled off his pig pen boots, slipped into his sneakers, wrapped a few clothes in a blanket and climbed back out the window. Running in the shadow of the house, he made it to the tool shed undetected. Now, running past the old threshing machine parked behind the tool shed, he approached the far side of the pond. He stashed his dry clothes and runners and stripped off his soiled, bloody shirt and pants. He pushed them under a rotten log and quietly submerged himself into the cool water of the pond to wash the grime off his body and emerge a new boy. Without making a sound, he dried himself with the blanket and climbed into the dry clothes. He tied up his sneakers, tossed the tied shut blanket over his shoulder, and headed for the railroad tracks. As soon as he cleared the fencerow and was out of sight and sound of the homestead, he ran like the wind. He wasn't sure where he was going, but he knew he had to run.

If I talk to Eve, Hugo will kill me. If I talk to the Sheriff, he'll wonder about the blood on my shirt. Hugo will say that I killed her. Besides, I can't even talk!

Run, Tommy, run!

Silo Boy on the Run

Tom ran for a mile or two, through the corn field, now high enough to hide even a six foot man, over the second cutting clover crop, through the young maple grove until he thought he would die from exhaustion, and fell behind an old bent up culvert pipe. A new pipe extended under the railroad tracks. His heart pounded in his chest and his head felt like a ripe pumpkin ready to burst. On hands and knees, he crawled through the new culvert and heard truck traffic coming from the interstate. Looking in all directions, he spotted a rest stop about a mile away. Weaving his way through the tall slough grass in the ditch beside the highway, he came to an opening where he could survey the situation at the rest stop. Cars were coming and going, but two trucks were parked at the truck stop some distance from the rest of the traffic. One truck had a licence plate from Pennsylvania and the other, a plate from Oklahoma. Both drivers were sleeping. The truck from Oklahoma pulled a flatbed trailer, its cargo covered with a large tarp. Tom decided to go west.

Tom got as close to the truck as possible from the cover of the ditch and then rather nonchalantly walked up to the flatbed and proceeded to take a leak behind the middle set of wheels. This would raise no suspicion if someone saw him, but it gave him time to check the scene. When all of the cars cleared out, he stepped up onto the hub of one of the wheels, tossed up his belongings, and then swung a leg onto the flatbed. He pulled his body beside the tarp, rolled under and nearly fainted from fright. When he could start breathing again and his eyes adjusted to the darkness, he was pleased to discover several large rolls of carpet. He worked his way along the rolls, squeezed in between them, placed his bag of things under his head and in no time was fast asleep.

Tom woke up to the roar of the diesel engine, but couldn't see a thing. The truck started to move and Tom could see the flash of lights as the truck met and passed cars on the interstate.

I don't know where I'm going, but at least I got away from Hugo and the police.

After a fitful sleep, filled with nightmares of Joyce, Tom remembered the nice things she did for him. He loved to read and Joyce made sure he had lots of reading material. The shelves were full of books and he could read them all. She also helped him with his speaking problem. She realized his potential and tried to nourish his keen mind. Soon Tom realized the driver was gearing down and pulling off the interstate.

What will happen if he checks his load? Should I run? Where will I go?

Tom heard the truck door slam shut and then lifted one corner of the tarp enough to see truck stop lights through the early morning fog.

I didn't realize I was so hungry and thirsty. Maybe I can get something from the garbage bin behind the restaurant. That way I won't have to talk to anyone. I wish I could talk normal.

With great care, Tom crawled out from under the tarp and climbed down from the flatbed on the side facing away from the restaurant. He again took a leak by the middle wheels and surveyed the scene through the fog. The country was unfamiliar and didn't seem to have a lot of hiding places. There were no trees, just flat grassland. He walked steadily around the truck and headed for the garbage bin.

If someone stops me, I'll just say I'm riding with the truck driver and we're collecting pop cans. Great! Here is half a burger and a part bottle of orange juice. I'll put a couple apples in my pocket.

It seemed like a long walk back to the truck. No place to hide. Finally, he reached the far side of the flatbed and climbed up to the tarp. Just as he lifted it to crawl under, the driver came around the front of the truck and started yelling.

"What do you think you're doing on my truck? Get out of there!"

Ooo! I'm hooped. The restaurant!

Tom ran for the back of the flatbed. It was a long way down, but he took a leap. Bouncing on one knee when he hit the ground, he recovered his balance and ran for the building. A teenaged boy had just come out the back door with the garbage. Tom grabbed his hat, ran through the door, and slammed it shut behind him. He blended in with the workers making eggs, hash browns and bacon. It was the morning rush hour with everyone demanding their food now. The cooks, waiters and cashiers were going crazy. It was easy to get lost in the crowd.

Oh no! The trucker!

Some people were just leaving their booth and Tom slid in, slouched down and started eating the leftover breakfast.

"Did you see a kid run through here?" The trucker yelled.

No one seemed to care about some kid on the run.

Just then Tom's face appeared on the big TV screen. It showed him in his barn clothes, stained with blood and his hands covered in dry blood. The announcer related the story about a kid that was wanted for questioning in the death of a woman from Indiana.

"That's the kid!" the trucker yelled. "He was hiding on my truck and he ran in here."

"There he is! He's got my cap on," the young man yelled.

Tom ran for the door, but there was nowhere to hide. The trucker grabbed him as Tom tripped over a big lady with a fresh breakfast tray. He and the trucker both landed on the floor, along with the bacon.

Silo Boy Returns

On the way home, Chad tried to converse with Tom, but Tom played the role of the deaf and dumb boy. He was locked in the back seat, separated from the driver by a metal mesh. With permission from the state to escort the witness back to Indiana, Chad talked away, as if to himself and a phantom passenger.

"It doesn't make any sense. How did Joyce end up in the well? Did she try to kill herself? She and her sister were close, and Eve insists Joyce would have given some indication if she were going to do more than run away. What do you think kid? Did you kill her?"

Silence from the back seat.

"It doesn't seem like it will make much difference, but you should be informed that anything said here could be used in a court of law."

Silence from the back seat.

"Hugo says she probably drowned herself, but I wonder if she was dead before she hit the water. What do you think, kid? Was that her blood on your shirt? Your name's Tom, right?"

Silence from the back seat. Chad continued talking, not revealing all of the information for this case.

He's hoping I'll talk. No way.

"Sometimes I wish we had a video of things that take place in situations like this, then we could just push replay and we'd know exactly what happened," Chad continued talking. "All we have now are two witnesses. One says he knows nothing about it and is back at the farm. The other one can't hear and can't talk. You're not blind too, are you Tom? What did you see?"

Silence from the back seat.

Crossing the state line, Chad announced, "Now we're home."

Tom looked at the familiar corn fields and the woods of Maple, Oak and Walnut, but kept silent. He was looking for a chance to run, but there was none.

"I don't know how a kid like you could kill a nice old lady like Joyce, but you sure had a lot of blood on you," Chad continued. "At least that's what showed on some pictures. You don't have them on now. I wonder where they are."

Silence from the back seat.

"If we had those clothes, we could type the blood to see if it matched with that of Joyce. We still haven't found a murder weapon, so we'll go back to the farm and have a look around."

Silence from the back seat, but the wheels of Tom's brain were running in high gear. As the police car turned onto the gravel road and headed up the driveway to the farm, Tom realized he might be meeting Hugo again.

"What will he do to me? I haven't talked, but he will blame me for pointing to the well. He said he would kill me, but I have to get to the log by the pond. The blood on my clothes is mine, not from Joyce. If they match the blood type, it will prove I didn't kill her. I have to get those clothes.

Tom winced and pointed to the outhouse.

"Okay, just a quick trip," Chad offered.

The back door of the police car swung open and Tom walked around the back of the house to the outhouse. As soon as he got behind the house he bolted for the fencerow and headed around the back of the barnyard to the pond. Chad watched from a distance, but didn't pursue. Two deputies had been called in and were across the road.

"Hey boy!" he heard Hugo bellow. "You gonna die just like Joyce. They'll find your skinny bag of bones under water and think you drowned yourself because you didn't want to go to jail for murder."

Hugo charged the boy and swept him into the pond. His strong arms wrapped around Tom and he held him face down in the water until Tom's lungs were bursting and he just had to exhale. However, with his exhale, he kicked his strong leg back through the muddy water and caught the big man right in the balls. Immediately, he felt the arms lose their grip on his shoulders as the big man doubled over in pain. Tom gasped for air, taking in a mouthful of putrid water as well. Both man and boy were spewing water and choking on the grime when Chad arrived.

Hugo tried to pull himself out of the mud and run off, but Chad called the two deputies and they handcuffed him.

"Take Hugo to the station, I'll look after Tom."

Dripping wet and shaking with fear, Tom nearly fainted and just sat down by an old log.

"Okay kid, I know you can talk. Eve told me. Maybe you have trouble, but you can talk. Take it slow. I want to know everything."

"I-I-I d-d-didn't k-k-kill n-n-nobody!" Tom sputtered.

"We know that," Chad said softly.

"H-H-He t-t-tried t-t-to kill me and make it look like I drownded myself," Tom sputtered between sobs.

"It's okay. He won't hurt anybody for a long time. He'll be doing time for first degree murder. Hugo said Joyce drowned herself, but the autopsy showed she died from a broken neck several hours before she went into the water."

Tom lost it completely now and just bawled. He cried for Joyce. He cried because he didn't help her. He cried because he didn't tell anybody what he knew. He cried with relief because he didn't drown and no longer had to fear Hugo. He just cried.

After Tom gained his composure, Chad asked, "Where are your bloody clothes?"

Tom reached around behind the log and pulled out the soiled clothes. With a gloved hand, Chad placed them into a plastic container to be submitted as evidence at a later date.

"Sorry Tom, but we had to use you as bait to flush out Hugo. We knew he would try to kill you because you were the only witness. True to character, he went for you and we were able to nab him. We wouldn't have let you drown. Say, you have a wicked back kick. Nicely placed," Chad said with a smile. Even Tom cracked a smile. On the way back to the farm house, Tom filled Chad in on the details of the story as well as he could.

"That rascal Hugo mowed the lawn from the cellar to the well to remove the marks where he dragged the body. Eve's friend Ted is a big nuisance sometimes, but he takes good pictures and he has a picture showing evidence of the drag marks to the well. Here he is now."

Eve's Red Lincoln pulled into the driveway and as the dust settled, Ted extracted his tall, lanky body. His head sported a buzz cut and a smile that spread across his face.

"Hi guys," Chad said as they met. "Meet the new Tom." Tom wasn't sure what was going on.

"Tom, meet Eve and Ted Harrington. They are looking after Joyce's affairs."

"Hi Tom," Eve greeted. "Joyce's will gives us ownership of this place. Ted and I would love to have you come live with us, until everything is worked out. We'll show you our place and a room you can have, if you want. You can still come to the farm to look after the animals, if you like. I'm sure you don't want to miss out on cleaning the pig pen and chasing the pigeons." They all laughed. "We want you to stay with us, just don't run off. Okay?" She said this with a smile, but it had a sound of authority.

"N-no no k-k-kill pigeons," Tom stuttered.

"No kill pigeons," Ted offered. I'll show you how to take pictures of the birds in flight. Pigeons have beautiful colors that shine in the right light."

"I am a teacher," Eve continued talking. "I know Joyce was working with you on your speech problem and I will continue. We know you are a very bright boy and very well read. We think you can make a great writer and maybe someday, a great speaker."

"Okay Tom," Chad spoke to the boy. "How are you riding to town? Are you going in the back seat of the cruiser with me or with Eve and Ted in the Lincoln?"

Tom's face lit up like the landscape lights up at sunrise. A broad smile broke out across his face.

"I-I-I'll go in the Lincoln!"

Chapter 16
Bird in Hand

How would you like to get caught in a net and have someone stick you in a bag to carry you to a banding station? It might just ruffle your feathers, right?

This is exactly what happens to hundreds of songbirds every spring and fall at the Lesser Slave Lake Bird Observatory Banding Station. The banding station is operated by Lesser Slave Lake Bird Observatory (LSLBO) and the Boreal Centre for Bird Conservation. The Boreal Centre is housed in a modern building, built to specifications that qualify it as a LEED (Leadership in Energy and Environmental Design) Gold building. It houses offices of the Bird Observatory and Lesser Slave Lake Provincial Park; a laboratory facility for university research, and has a large room full of interactive displays about birds for school groups and the general public. The banding station is a small building located at an exceptionally beautiful location along the north shore of Lesser Slave Lake in Alberta, Canada.

One can hear the haunting laugh of a Loon in the distance as waves splash on the rocks along the shore. In the spring, the sun rises about 4:30 AM and the bird banders set up the nets for the day.

Who are bird banders? Richard is a bird bander. He also speaks to school groups.

"Do you have to be smart to be a bird bander?" a grade five student asks.

"Well," Richard says with a smile. "You need some training to band birds. It would be illegal for you to set up a net and catch birds in your backyard."

"Do you have to go to university?" another student asks.

"No, but I have a degree in Environmental and Conservation Science."

"What about you?" the student points to the assistant bander, Nicole.

"I have an Honours diploma in Renewable Resources."

"How old do you have to be?"

"There are some young bird banders, but most are adults who have degrees and special training. Let's see if we can find some birds," Richard says as he starts leading the class toward the net lanes.

"Do you need a license?"

"Yes. The bird observatory has a master permit and we have sub-permit banding licenses under this master permit. I have a sub-permit to work with songbirds."

"I also have a sub-permit under the master permit," Nicole offered.

"Did it take a long time?"

"We had to take special training, and then pass a test where two expert banders watched us work with birds," Nicole answered. "We also needed to identify all of the birds in the area by sight and sound."

"Was it scary?"

"Yes," Richard said with a chuckle.

"Are you going to go back to school?"

"Someday, I may go for a Master's degree," Richard answered.

"Could I be a bander?"

"With proper training, anyone can be a bird bander, even you."

"We have to check the nets!" Nicole called from a net lane.

Richard and Nicole continued giving information to the class.

"We use leg bands to collect information about migrating birds. All of the information is recorded on special data sheets. Later it will be entered into a computer and sent to the US Department of Fish and Wildlife in Laurel, Maryland," Richard told the class.

"This information will be used to learn more about these amazingly beautiful birds that migrate thousands of kilometres each year," Nicole continued.

"Where do they travel?" a student asked.

Other students ask, "How fast do they fly?"

"How do they find their way?"

"Why have their numbers drastically dropped in recent years?"

"These are some of the questions bird banders are trying to answer," Richard explained.

The banders related that many birds migrate at night, including the small, colourful songbirds. Some are long-distance, neotropical migrants. In the early morning, they land in the willow shrubs growing along the edge of the lake to feed and rest. Scientists have found Slave Lake to be an excellent site for a banding station, since these birds follow the lake shore as they travel north to nest in the spring, and pass by again in the fall, as they travel south for the winter. Some will stay during the spring and summer, nesting in the boreal forest around Slave Lake.

Long narrow clearings called net lanes are cut through the bushes. Black, lightweight, nylon mist nets are stretched the length of the lane and hung between two aluminum poles. One to twelve net lanes may be used depending on the weather and the wind.

"How does weather affect banding?" a student asked.

"If the birds get wet from hanging too long in the rain, they could get chilled and then get sick or die," Richard explained.

Nicole continued to explain that, "A net, swinging in the wind, will alert a bird to danger and they will just fly around or over it."

There are many different kinds of song birds, and in the spring the males usually exhibit a blaze of colour, as they fly north to mate and nest. They also have a variety of songs and calls to identify their territory and to attract a mate. Some birds fly into the nets and get their wings and feet caught.

"We must gently untangle feet, legs, wings and head," Richard said, as he held a tiny bird with its head between his first and second fingers. His thumb and third finger held the bird's legs and feet. He was very careful not to injure the bird, especially its fragile legs.

"This is called extracting," Nicole said, and some days we extract over two hundred birds caught in the nets. We must work fast, yet carefully, to band all of the birds."

"What do you do next?" a student asked.

Richard continued his explanation. "When completely free of the net, the bird is placed into a small cloth bag with a draw string that can be pulled to close the opening. The dark environment inside of the bag helps calm the captured bird."

While talking excitedly about the birds caught, Richard and Nicole collected and labeled the bags. This identified the specific net lane where the bird was caught. When taking the birds back to the small building for banding, everyone was looking and listening for other birds.

"What bird is singing now?" someone asked

"Look, there he is."

"What is it?"

"Look at the geese flying over the lake."

"There is a Bald Eagle," Nicole said as she pointed to a large bird with a white head and white tail, soaring over the lake.

Back at the banding building, the first step was to take the bird out of the bag as quickly as possible. The birds were positively identified by checking the size, colour, and specific markings for each species.

"What is that?" a student asked.

"This is a small aluminum band we place on one leg, using this special kind of pliers to prevent injury to the bird." Nicole explained.

"Each band has a different number and is recorded for future identification," Richard said. "When the bird already has a band from some other banding station, we get pretty excited."

While Nicole explained the procedures to the interested visitors, Richard checked the fat deposit and muscle development by blowing on the feathers under the neck. Wing length was measured with a micrometre. This information was recorded by a volunteer. Feathers were also checked for condition and wear.

"If the bird is a male, he is checked for a cloacal protuberance," Richard said, as he blew on the belly of a bird. "Blowing on his bottom separates the feathers to expose his cloaca. A swelling of this organ indicates he is ready for mating. If the bird is a female, she is checked for a brood patch on her breast." Again Richard blew on the feathers to expose the patch.

"During the nesting season, this area loses its feathers and becomes filled with blood vessels. The blood filled exposed patch helps to warm the eggs in the nest during incubation," Nicole added.

"By looking at the wing feathers," Nicole continued, "we can estimate the age of a bird. To age a young bird, we use a procedure called skulling. This is done by using a wet finger to push apart the feathers on top of the head. A juvenile will have a soft spot, much like a human baby. An adult does not."

With a big smile, Richard now checked the weight of the bird by placing it head first into an empty plastic tube and weighing it on an electronic balance. The weight is measured to one tenth of a gram. A kinglet, for example, may weigh as little as six grams, the weight of a quarter.

When the bander is finished, the bird is admired and photographed by the visitors. Then the hand that held the bird is opened. Sometimes the bird leaves a little deposit on the hand before it flies off, as if to say "pooh on you!"

Feathers are ruffled, but otherwise the birds are unharmed. Soon they will get back to the business of courting, mating and nesting. Some, however, will be sporting a ring on their leg and a new, fancy hair-do.

While waiting for the next round of collecting birds, the students peppered the banders with many interesting questions.

"How many birds have you banded?"

"A total of 55,255 birds and over 100 different species have been banded since the beginning of the LSLBO in1993," Richard answered.

"What's the biggest bird you've banded?"

"The Northern Goshawk. It is the largest forest hawk with a wingspan of 75 centimetres and it weighs about one kilogram."

"What's the smallest bird you've banded?"

"The smallest bird we've banded is a kinglet. We've caught a hummingbird, but we are not allowed to band them. We just let them go."

"What's the meanest bird?"

"Well, the woodpeckers can hurt you, when they drill you with their bills. The talons of the Sharp-shinned Hawk can tear your skin off, but for its size, the Black-capped Chickadee is the greatest fighter," Nicole answered with a smile.

"What's the oldest bird you've caught?"

"Aging birds is very difficult, but we banded an Alder Flycatcher in 1996 and it was recaptured here in 2005 so it was at least 10 years old. Most birds don't live that long."

"How fast do birds fly?"

"The fastest bird is a Red-breasted Merganser that can fly 161 kilometres an hour!"

'Wow!"

"Time to check the nets!" Richard announced.

If you want to learn more, stop by the banding station and ask Richard and Nicole.

Maybe someday the banding information that Richard, Nicole and other banders are collecting will answer the questions we have about migrating songbirds. We already know that some of the decline in the number of birds is caused by a loss of nesting habitat in the boreal forest of the north, and wintering habitat in the tropical rain forest. Other reasons may include hurricanes, tornadoes, crashing into high rise buildings, wind turbines, electric wires and natural predators, as well as the friendly, household cat.

More answers to questions about the decline of songbirds may give information about the environmental changes that are also affecting humans. Hopefully, the answers will come before it is too late for both birds and humans.

If you are looking for an interesting excursion, try a visit to the Boreal Centre for Bird Conservation and the Lesser Slave Lake Bird Observatory Banding Station. However, don't get caught in a net. You might end up with more than ruffled feathers!

*Based on an interview with Richard Krikun and Nicole Linfoot, banders at the LSLBO.

Chapter 17
Y3K

Y3K Alert! Y3K Alert!

"Check the PTM," (Personal Telecommunication Monitor) Luna told his father as they were rocketing through space in their VTD (Virtual Transportation Device). The two just attained cruising speed after their take off from Chicago. They locked into UTS (Universe Travel Systems) and Father was ready to relax.

The monitor speakers screamed.

Y3K Alert! Y3K Alert!

"Bunk!" Father snarled. "Just more alarmist propaganda."

"But Father," Luna protested. "The Y3K virus could infect all of our navigation and communication systems. Switching from 2999 to year 3000 could be a disaster."

Y3K Alert! Y3K Alert!

With a blink of his eye, Father switched channels to AMS, the Agricultural Monitoring System.

Father managed a vast agricultural complex in northern Illinois. By checking the AMS, he could get the most recent data on the corn crop. A complete data system collected and analyzed all of the current information on temperature, relative humidity and the kernel moisture index. When the monitor flashed Harvest, Father would push a button and massive ARHs (Automatic Robotic Hovercraft) would begin the harvest of genetically engineered corn grown on perfectly flat fields with no weeds, trees or shrubs. The corn was genetically engineered to produce its own individualized fertilizer, along with effective and efficient pesticides and herbicides.

"Are we there yet?" Luna asked.

"Another ten minutes," Father replied.

"Did they have Disney Universe when you were a kid?"

"No, it's only been open for three years."

"My friend Aster said the RBTU (Ride Between the Universes) is the greatest."

Luna and his father Simoon were taking a short holiday to Disney Universe before harvest time. It was also one of the field excursions required for Luna's course of study at City Virtual Learning Centre in Rockford.

Y3K Alert! Y3K Alert!

Luna saw the alert on the surround monitor. He clicked onto the virtual sound modem, careful not to alert Father. No worry. Father was dozing on his reclining travel sofa.

"Who are you?" Luna gasped as a face appeared on the screen. No answer.

Adjusting the earth monitor, Luna focused on a young boy named Robert sitting in the passenger seat of a giant corn picker. Robert's father made adjustments to the cabin climate control. Ninety degrees Fahrenheit outside, but a cool, dust free seventy degrees Fahrenheit inside. The picker, guided by a GPS (Global Positioning System), devoured long rows of corn and separated the kernels from the cobs. This was harvest time in Illinois, 1999.

"What's on TV?" Robert's Father asked, pointing to the in-cab TV.

"There's a program about Y2K," Robert responded. "It's pretty scary. They say all of our telecommunication systems will fail when we change from year 1999 to year 2000. Computers will crash, security systems will fail and there will be riots and wars.

"What's new?" father said sarcastically. "Turn that crap off! It's just a bunch of propaganda bunk by alarmist extremists."

Just then the face of a young boy appeared on the screen. Robert adjusted the set. Father was busy running the picker and wouldn't listen anyway.

"What is this?" Robert questioned as he focused on a father and his son struggling with a huge root.

"Bring the mule," Father called to Harold.

Harold was fourteen years old on this day in 1920. He and his father were clearing the forest to make new cropland. A small plot of corn struggled to grow around the many stumps.

The field was surrounded by massive oak trees, all part of the original northern Illinois forest. As homesteaders, Harold's family was trying to grow enough corn to survive the winter. Stump by stump they cleared the forest.

"You know that Model T Ford that Uncle Evert has?" Harold asked his father. "If we had one of those, we could put two big drive wheels on the back. By adjusting the gears, I bet we could pull these stumps clean out of here."

"Dream on," father said as he reached for the lunch basket. "It's time for lunch. You hungry?"

After lunch, Father leaned up against a stump and dozed off. Harold looked up and saw two Bald Eagles soaring high above.

"Someday I'll fly like those eagles!"

"Dream on," he said to himself, not waiting for Father's usual reply.

Flash! Flash!

"What is this? Who are you"?

In the distance, Harold saw a Native American boy, and his father crouching beside a towering oak tree. Sabbachese and his father were skinning a deer they had killed with a bow and arrow. They had no guns, so this must have been from a time before the white explorers.

"Why do we save the brains?" Sabbachese asked his father. "Will they make us wiser?"

"We use every part of an animal," Father replied. "The brains will be used to tan the hide. The meat will be dried to make pemmican and the tanned hide will give us new robes for the winter. If we wear the robes long enough, we'll be able to travel between many worlds in the future."

Sabbachese wondered how that would take place, but it was best not to ask too many questions.

"I'm sure it will be exciting," he replied, as he continued to stir the deer brains.

"Buckle up!" Father startled Luna. "We're making our descent into Disney Universe. I'm sure you'll have a great time today, Luna."

After the final approach and landing, the pair was virtually transported to the main lobby. No crowds in a virtual lobby.

"You go ahead and enjoy all of the rides," Father said. "I'll pay with my iris scan."

"Come on Father! You'll miss all of the fun!"

"That's okay. I have to watch the Agricultural Monitoring System in case it's time for the harvest."

"I'm going to try the RBTU (Ride Between the Universes) first," Luna called to his father.

It will have to be pretty amazing to beat what I saw on the way here!

Luna hurried off to be virtually transported onto the RBTU.

I hope there are no Y3K problems on the way!

Made in the USA
Charleston, SC
13 June 2014